This book belongs to

....

....

....

First published 2019 by Johnny Magory Business.
Ballynafagh, Prosperous, Naas, Co. Kildare, Ireland

ISBN: 978-0-9935792-6-4

Text, Illustrations, Design © 2019 Emma-Jane Leeson
www.JohnnyMagory.com

This book was produced entirely in Ireland
(and we're really proud about that!)

Written by Emma-Jane Leeson, Kildare
Edited by Aoife Barrett, Dublin
Illustrations by Don Conroy, Wicklow
Colouring and Graphic Design by Nicola Sedgwick, Wicklow

Printed by KPS Colour Print, Mayo

Proud Partners of CMRF Crumlin.
2% of proceeds from the sale of this book will be donated to this charity.
Please visit **www.CMRF.org** for more information.

**The Children's Medical
& Research Foundation**
Our Lady's Children's
Hospital, Crumlin

Johnny Magory

and the Forest Fleadh Cheoil

Emma-Jane Leeson

For
Lily Leeson & May Ivers
– Thank you both for inspiring five generations . . .
and many more to come x

I'll tell you a story about Johnny Magory,

His sister Lily-May and their trusty dog Ruairi.

The clever two are five and eight years old,

They're **usually** good

but they're

sometimes **bold!**

One of their favourite places to go is their local park,
To play amongst the trees and plants, from daylight through to dark.

They pack a picnic and a ball and change into their best exploring gear,
To wander along the paths and forest trails that they love so dear.

Ma finds the **perfect spot** on the grass to set up for the day,

They play some football with their friends and Ruairi leads the way.

And when the game has finished, they **dig** into their yummy food,

Tasty baked brown bread and cheddar cheese **really sets the mood.**

Ma and Da lie back to **read** their books and **relax** into their day,

Johnny and Lily-May explore the park with Ruairi, where it's safe to play.

Around the yew tree, down by the lake,

near the **CASTLE RUIN** to their hidden place,

A circular clearing surrounded by giant beech trees

– a really magic space.

Walking through the undergrowth, Lily-May spots Kyran the deer,

They **gallop** over to him and Kyran says, "Didn't you hear?

Today's the day for our **Fleadh Cheoil**, I've been practising all week!"

"My bodhran's sounding really sweet," he says, with an excited "eek!"

A Fleadh Cheoil is a music competition for every musician,

They play **Irish tunes** on their instruments, a really special tradition.

'Go hiontach!' Johnny shouts, taking his tin whistle in his hand,

'I've practised loads of jigs and reels really hard with my school band.'

'I hear them!' says Lily May, flying through the whispering leaves,

She PULLS back a holly bush and is amazed by what she sees.

Meabh fox is playing **fiddle**,
while Caoimhe red squirrel tunes her **harp**,
Joseph badger plays **accordion**
and practises his **flats** and **sharps**.

Layla barn owl sits high up in the tree and listens with a keen ear,

She's the Fleadh Cheoil judge and will carefully score every tune she hears.

Thalia kestrel takes centre stage

and plays the great

Cooley's Reel,

Lily-May set dances with Oliver duck tapping on her heel.

Johnny climbs high up the giant oak to sit with Layla barn owl,
And as Danny robin plays the spoons, Ruairi dances with a howl.

Next Brayson
field mouse on his flute
steals the show,
playing a hornpipe.
Everyone dances between
the trees and shouts out,
"Fleadh is the life!"
Hayden pine marten belts out a jig
on his trusty Irish uilleann pipes,
Tiny Rihanna wren
dances along
showing off her delicate
feathered stripes.

Ben crow **slows things down** when he sings 'Róisín Dubh', an old sean-nós song,
Then Joey magpie plays his shiny whistle to bring the beat back along.

Layla owl announces the winner and Meabh fox squeals 'Ar fheabhas!' with delight.

Fleadh Cheoil is over and they all say 'Slán,' but then Johnny gets a FRIGHT —

He's climbed so high up the massive oak tree; he really can't see his way down.

"You need to save the day, Lily-May," he yells to his sister on the ground.

Okay, Ruairi and I will get Ma and Da,
be careful not to fall.
Come on, Ruairi, let's run quickly,
we're on an ADVENTURE after all.

At home that evening after supper Johnny reads aloud Lily-May's favourite book,

'The owl who couldn't give a hoot',

as they're curled up in their cosy reading nook.

Ma and Da climb up to Johnny
and help him to **come down** to the ground.
Then they spend the afternoon
playing in the oak,
swinging around and round.

They speed back through the undergrowth and by the castle ruin,

Down by the lake, around the yew,

They'll be there really soon.

"Ma! Da! You need to come quickly, Johnny's stuck in the oak tree!"

"I told him not to climb too high," Da says. "Come on, let's go see."